A GOLDEN WHEELS BOOK
Dirt Bikes
Scramblers/Enduros/Trials/Motocross

RAY HILL

Photography by DOUG MELLOR

GOLDEN PRESS / NEW YORK
Western Publishing Company, Inc., Racine, Wisconsin

Motorcycles courtesy Ashford Engineering, Cosmopolitan Motors, Devon Honda, GKR, Herdan Corporation, Larry's Triumph, Puch International, Simpson's Harley-Davidson, Westchester Honda, YBM Cycle Sales.

Library of Congress Catalog Card Number: 74-77914

Foreword

Dirt bikes are among the most specialized vehicles ever designed. Intended either solely or primarily for off-road riding, they are personifications of pure function, from their knobby tires to their waterproof air filters to their unbreakable plastic fenders. But there are as many kinds of dirt motorcycles as there are varieties of off-road riding, and each excels at different tasks.

If you just want to meander slowly through open fields, or down smooth dirt roads, then all you need is a low-speed, small-displacement machine without any particular pretensions in the handling department. If you should want to try something more demanding, you'll need a more sophisticated machine. Perhaps you'd like to be able to ride on paved highways in order to get to your favorite fireroad. Then you're going to need lighting equipment and a horn so that the state will grant you a registration, and once you're out there on the highway you'll need to keep up with traffic. Which means a higher top speed than many low-geared dirt bikes can attain. So you're talking about a dual-purpose machine, probably something near 250cc, that will give you the necessary speed.

If you expect to be off the road most of the time, then high top speed and lighting equipment are of secondary importance. Except if you're an enduro rider. For the specialized type of off-road competition known as an enduro, lighting equipment is required in case the competitors have to cross a highway getting from one forest trail to another. But in no way is an enduro a true dual-purpose machine. It's made for averaging maybe 20 miles an hour through woods and streams, sand and marshes and all sorts of outlandish terrain. Accordingly, the prime emphasis is on reliability and low-speed power to drag the rider through the rough stuff.

Even slower, more impossible going requires a more specialized machine. And that gets into another form of competition, called trials. Trials sections resemble miniature versions of the Grand Canyon—and the competitors are expected to ride up the nearly perpendicular slope. Points are deducted if their feet touch the ground even once, so trials bikes are the epitome of poise under slow, slow conditions. A good trials rider can balance almost motionless on a steep hillside covered with slippery mud and make a quick 90-degree turn over a fallen tree trunk at the same time. He has to have a pretty agile machine under him to perform tricks like that.

For carving through the woods and streams over long periods of time, the ISDT type of enduro bike has evolved over the years.

These machines have to do everything an enduro bike can do—and
nearly everything a trials bike can do—but do it for six days at a
stretch. The regulations of the International Six Day Trial stipulate
that the riders must do all their own maintenance during the race,
so ISDT bikes are equipped with tool kits, spare parts and usually
such refinements as rear wheels that detach quickly for tire changing by one man, two complete electrical systems—just in case—
unbreakable fenders and other durable components so that the inevitable fall won't mean mechanical disaster.

    At the other extreme of long-distance competition are the big
desert races—such as the Baja 1000 and Mint 400—where all-out
top speed through sandy terrain is required. The bikes have to handle, but more often in the 70 mph to 90 mph range than the 10 mph
to 50 mph bracket in which enduro bikes operate. The biggest desert racers—501 Maicos, 400 Husqvarnas—will run over 100 mph
through sandy wasteland for 15 to 20 hours at a stretch. While desert
racing is just as demanding as ISDT competition, the parameters
are all different, and the bike configuration differs accordingly.

    Different again are motocross machines. Top speeds need to be
fairly high, but more important are handling and quick acceleration.

Motocross tracks are hilly dirt circuits, rutted and potholed as you might expect from dozens of motorcycles roaring around as fast as possible, often spending nearly as much time bouncing through the air as clawing at the ground.

There are smoother versions of motocross tracks which demand nearly the same qualities but require less ground clearance because of fewer bumps. Machines for these tracks often show up with low exhausts—not unlike those on street motorcycles—smaller tires and wheels and other minor differences. On the flatter tracks, the bikes spend a good portion of the race sliding sideways around corners, just as the big custom-built mile and half-mile dirt trackers do.

Out of all the dirt bikes that are available, most riders end up either with enduro machines—because they go perfectly well in the woods and can also be safely driven on paved roads—or low-key motocross bikes that handle well enough to cover most sorts of terrain rapidly enough to suit the majority of off-road riders. The very specialized machines, logically enough, aren't as popular, because their use is more limited. But the various types of off-road riding are so demanding, and so varied, that specific bikes are almost always necessary for specific purposes. □

Benelli

Benelli Enduro 175

Engine: Two-stroke Single
7:1 compression ratio, 60x60mm, 170cc
Ignition: Flywheel magneto
Transmission: 4-speed **Wheelbase:** 51.5 in
Ground Clearance: 9.75 in **Weight:** 210 lbs

Benelli has been building motorcycles since 1914, always in small quantities and always with superlative craftsmanship. Now owned by Alejandro De Tomaso—creator of the Pantara sports coupe—the firm offers a complete line of motorcycles. The only true dirt bike among them, however, is the Enduro 175. And even it is a dual-purpose machine, equally useful for basic street transportation.

The Enduro has all the right equipment, including Marzocchi front suspension and rear shock absorbers, Pirelli motocross tires, quick-detach lighting and an extremely upswept exhaust that comes as high as the tank. There is even a sturdy skid plate. The 4-speed gearbox suffers from a deficiency of ratios, and the little two-stroke Single requires messy mixing of oil with the gas, as there is no provision for automatic oiling. But if a simple, well-built, conventional Italian dirt machine is what you're after, you can't beat the Benelli.

Bombardier virtually invented the modern snowmobile, and this Valcourt, Quebec, firm has recently applied its advanced technology to the motorcycle. The result is an excellent dirt bike, available in 125cc and 175cc versions. The 175 is the hot setup, however, for it will outrun most 350s. The secret is the rotary-valve Single built by Rotax, a firm more famous until now for its equally powerful snowmobile engines. A 6-speed gearbox allows you to select a ratio for any contingency, and hefty amounts of torque will pull you out of whatever emergency you manage to get yourself into.

The rest of the Can-Am seems to work equally well, and while the components are not particularly innovative, the total machine is more than competitive in every way. The Bombardier is strikingly styled, with modern graphics on the tank and side covers, and it seems taut and precise. A number of Can-Ams have been winning races with remarkable consistency, attesting to the bike's all-round desirability for off-road riding.

Bombardier

Bombardier Can-Am 175

Engine: Two-stroke Single
13:1 compression ratio, 62x57.5mm, 173.6cc
Ignition: Capacitive discharge
Transmission: 6-speed **Wheelbase:** 54 in
Ground Clearance: 9 in **Weight:** 233 lbs

Bultaco

Bultaco is a dream company in many ways, a private concern sequestered in the Spanish mountains and run by Señor Francisco Bulto and his family—including his young motorcyclist daughter. There is nothing provincial about Bultaco, however, for the patron's enthusiasm and skill assure that every model meets his own demanding standards. And while all Bultacos use the same well-proved piston-port, two-stroke Single—in various displacements and states of tune—there is incredible diversity within the Bultaco range.

Two very specialized models—the Matador S-D and the Astro 250—appear in this country only infrequently. The Matador is aimed at winning the ISDT, and carries all the necessary gear—tire pumps, tools and hordes of spares—to qualify for International Six Day Trial competition. The Astro is a short-track racer, meant for racing half-mile dirt tracks and the Houston Astrodome indoor race from which it takes its name. Unless you're a professional racer, you really don't need either.

For the general market, Bultaco's line is simplicity itself. There are three models, each aimed at a specific dirt rider. The Alpina is

the enduro model—complete with lights and muffler—that also makes a decent trials bike. It's easily the most popular of all the Bultacos, and can be had in 125cc, 175cc, 250cc and 350cc sizes. The only difference is the bore. This means you can start out with a docile 125 and switch cylinder, head and piston to a more powerful size once you become more proficient.

Alpinas have a one-piece fiberglass seat and tank, alloy fenders, Betor suspension and high exhausts. There are no spark arrestors, though, and annoyingly, no oil injection. What there is, however, is sophisticated handling and substantial amounts of pulling power that can climb hills where mountain goats get breathless.

Bultaco Alpina 125

Engine: Two-stroke Single
10:1 compression ratio, 51.5x60mm, 125cc
Ignition: Flywheel magneto
Transmission: 5-speed **Wheelbase:** 52 in
Ground Clearance: 11 in **Weight:** 210 lbs

Bultaco Pursang 250

Engine: Two-stroke Single
12:1 compression ratio, 72x60mm, 244cc
Ignition: Capacitive discharge
Transmission: 5-speed **Wheelbase:** 56 in
Ground Clearance: 9 in **Weight:** 216 lbs

The Pursang is Bultaco's racing model. It's been fantastically successful at everything from long-distance desert races and scrambles to motocross and TT. Like the Alpina, it's available in four displacements, each one the ruler of its racing class. It features Betor suspension, a super-strong frame, Pirelli motocross knobbies and a downswept exhaust pipe with easily removable spring-loaded muffler. Major changes in carburetion, compression ratio and ignition give the Pursang models just about double the horsepower of equal displacement Alpinas. But in the flat-out racing at which they excel, that's what you need. And that's what Pursangs deliver.

The Sherpa T is Bultaco's trials model, and presently it comes only in 250cc and 350cc versions. Like other Bultacos, these are identical except for displacement and are superior to everything else in their class. The Sherpa T is easily the most popular trials bike available, for the simple reason that it will climb through impossible terrain better than anything else. Huge flywheels keep the low-horsepower/high-torque engine smooth and consistent for unbroken traction on difficult surfaces, while the long-travel front shocks and light alloy front wheel allow easy lofting over larger obstacles. All in all, the Sherpa T is the nearest thing to a perfect trials mount, despite the efforts of other manufacturers—particularly the Japanese—to excel in this increasingly popular domain.

Bultaco Sherpa T 350
Engine: Two-stroke Single
9:1 compression ratio, 83.2x60mm, 326cc
Ignition: Flywheel magneto
Transmission: 5-speed **Wheelbase:** 52 in
Ground Clearance: 12 in **Weight:** 209 lbs

CZ

Like Bultaco, this 45-year-old Czechoslovakian motorcycle factory fabricates a whole array of excellent racers by fitting different engine displacements into identical frames. You have your choice of 125cc, 250cc or 400cc versions, each one of which is a purebred, demanding and savage motocross racer of international caliber that requires experts-only ability.

The secret of CZ success is long years of competition on the rigorous European championship motocross circuit, coupled with extremely powerful engines. In order to get that peak output, however, most low-speed tractability is lost. Which makes using the CZ throttle much like clicking a switch—the power comes on in a surge. If you're expert enough to handle it, there are few faster ways around a championship dirt course.

CZ 400 Motocross

Engine: Two-stroke Single
10.5:1 compression ratio, 82x72mm, 380cc
Ignition: Flywheel magneto
Transmission: 4-speed **Wheelbase:** 55 in
Ground Clearance: 7.5 in **Weight:** 242 lbs

Aermacchi—Harley-Davidson's Italian subsidiary—makes a number of traditional Italian dirt machines ranging from 90cc to 350cc. Each one is different, and all are aimed at the dual-purpose market. The SR-100 Baja has been a really significant racer, but it lacks versatility. Only the SX-350 has captured the public imagination.

A horizontal four-stroke Single, Aermacchi's dirt bike is the last of what was once a popular configuration. It now comes with universal tires, high exhaust, good ground clearance, considerable torque . . . and electric starting. Unfortunately, it also weighs more than 350 pounds, which makes it heavier than many street machines of equal displacement. Serious dirt riding is out of the question, but on the other hand, a casual trip down a smooth fireroad isn't totally beyond comprehension.

Harley-Davidson

Harley-Davidson SX-350

Engine: Four-stroke Single
9.3:1 compression ratio, 74x80mm, 344cc
Ignition: Battery and coil
Transmission: 5-speed **Wheelbase:** 56 in
Ground Clearance: 7.5 in **Weight:** 355 lbs

Hodaka

Pabatco is a small importer in Athena, Oregon, that over a decade ago was stuck with a 90cc two-stroke engine built by associates in Japan, wrapped in a virtually unmarketable street bike. So they sent out 10,000 questionnaires asking U. S. riders what they wanted in a small off-road motorcycle. The result was the Hodaka Ace 90, one of the most successful small bikes ever built. In recent years, the basic package has been so improved that it's virtually unrecognizable, but the old virtues of simplicity, economy and reliability have been retained in the new models.

The present lineup includes four bikes—two each of 100cc and 125cc—that differ only in displacement and accessories. There are two enduro models and two motocross racers. All of them have more

Hodaka Dirt Squirt

Engine: Two-stroke Single
6.7:1 compression ratio, 50x50mm, 98cc
Ignition: Flywheel magneto
Transmission: 5-speed **Wheelbase:** 50 in
Ground Clearance: 9 in **Weight:** 185 lbs

Hodaka Combat Wombat

Engine: Two-stroke Single
8:1 compression ratio, 56x50mm, 123cc
Ignition: Flywheel magneto
Transmission: 5-speed **Wheelbase:** 53 in
Ground Clearance: 9.7 in **Weight:** 192 lbs

horsepower than you'd expect from their rudimentary engines, lots of ground clearance, excellent handling and handsome chrome gas tanks. The only thing they still don't have is oil injection, but they do feature 21-inch front wheels on the 125s, lots of alloy and extremely light weight. They're also saddled with names like Dirt Squirt, Super Rat and Combat Wombat, but you can't blame that on the motorcycles.

Honda

The giant Honda Motor Company produces such a profusion of machines, with models appearing and disappearing from the lineup like ducks in a shooting gallery, that it's almost impossible to keep them straight. There is a system to this madness, however. All you have to know is your prefixes, and everything comes out clear.

The prefix MT designates Honda's recent venture into two-stroke enduro bikes. These are powered by fairly conventional two-cycle Singles, and come in either 125cc or 250cc. Both versions are among the most powerful in their respective classes, and both are extremely light. Off-road performance is pretty impressive, for both handle very well and have excellent brakes. Things like a 21-inch front wheel, alloy tank, skid plate and other necessary bits are standard, and there is even street-legal quick-detach equipment—including lights, horn and turn signals. But the Honda MTs are certainly more at home in the boondocks than on the highway.

Honda MT-250

Engine: Two-stroke Single
6.6:1 compression ratio, 70x64.4mm, 248cc
Ignition: Flywheel magneto
Transmission: 5-speed **Wheelbase:** 56.5 in
Ground Clearance: 10 in **Weight:** 268 lbs

The motocross racing versions of the Honda MT-125 and MT-250 are the CR-125 and CR-250. Once again, these are ultra-light two-stroke Singles with reams of horsepower. The racers come complete with 18-inch knobby tires, alloy fuel tank, downswept expansion chamber and—unlike the MT enduro models, which enjoy the convenience of oil injection—require premixing of oil with the gasoline. If it helps to win races, that's okay though, and the lightweight Hondas win more than their share.

Honda CR-250 Elsinore

Engine: Two-stroke Single
7.2:1 compression ratio, 70x64.4mm, 248cc
Ignition: Flywheel magneto
Transmission: 5-speed   **Wheelbase:** 57 in
Ground Clearance: 7.5 in   **Weight:** 214 lbs

Honda XL-175

Engine: Four-stroke Single
9:1 compression ratio, 64x54mm, 174cc
Ignition: Battery and coil
Transmission: 5-speed **Wheelbase:** 53 in
Ground Clearance: 8 in **Weight:** 243 lbs

Honda also makes dirt bikes with four-stroke engines. Some of these are basically street bikes with a smattering of off-road accessories— the CL and SL series. The CLs are the more street-oriented of the two, and start with a 70cc Single. There are also a CL-100 and 125. Then come the two-cylinder CL-175 and CL-350 . . . and a similar 450 Twin built around the double overhead cam CB-450 powerplant. The slightly more sporting SL series includes a 100cc Single, a 125cc Single and a 350cc Twin. All of these machines serve overlapping purposes, and all can be considered primarily off-road playbikes.

There are also some serious Honda four-stroke Singles for true off-road use. These are known as the XL series, and start with the fine 175. It uses an engine derived from the 125 models and features a downswept tucked-in exhaust, a high front fender, 21-inch front wheel, street-legal electrics and a host of other refinements. Top speed is over 70 mph, and the 5-speed transmission lets you use lots of low-speed torque besides.

Along with the XL-175, Honda makes a 250 model—with four valves to feed its Single cylinder and a raft of other nice features. The first of Honda's serious dirt bikes, the 250 has been successful as both an enduro racer and a playbike. A number of early machines were even modified for motocross and did fairly well before Honda's competitive two-stroke racers appeared.

The top of the Honda dirt line is the XL-350, and like the other four-strokers it has a single overhead cam and four valves. This also has full street equipment, but only in the interests of legality. Its true vocation is as an off-road playbike or a slightly overweight enduro mount. It has wonderful low-speed pulling power, yet the top speed approaches 90 mph. The XL-350 is a legitimate four-stroke dirt bike with dual-purpose performance—a difficult combination to find these days.

Honda XL-350

Engine: Four-stroke Single
8.3:1 compression ratio, 79x71mm, 348cc
Ignition: Flywheel magneto
Transmission: 5-speed **Wheelbase:** 55.5 in
Ground Clearance: 8.5 in **Weight:** 307 lbs

Husqvarna

For a number of years, Husqvarna absolutely ruled long-distance off-road racing, with the inevitable result that other manufacturers have improved their own products to narrow the gap. These days, the gap is smaller than ever, but the Swedish Huskies are still consistently the top racers, day in and day out.

The latest model is the 125 MX, which shares many components with the larger bikes. Incredible sophistication has been brought to the design of the minor details that combine to make a winning bike, with things like unbreakable plastic fenders, low-resistance straight-cut primary gears, high-quality Reynolds drive chain, a chrome-moly frame, Akront alloy rims, Betor suspension and an adjustable gearshift lever that can be fitted to either side.

All Huskies have more than enough horsepower, fine handling and versatile characteristics that allow them to excel in most types of competition. If you're a racer, a Husky is hard to beat.

Husqvarna 125 MX

Engine: Two-stroke Single
13:1 compression ratio, 55x52mm, 124cc
Ignition: Capacitive discharge
Transmission: 6-speed **Wheelbase:** 53 in
Ground Clearance: 8 in **Weight:** 205 lbs

Like most other manufacturers, Husqvarna sells a full line of bikes in different displacements, achieved by slightly modifying the basic machine. In the 250cc class, it manufactures a motocrosser, an enduro model and a desert sled, each one based on the same general configuration, with minimal changes to gearing and suspension to adapt it to a specific type of racing. There is also a 360cc enduro bike with street-legal equipment and a 400cc motocross machine of similar specification.

The most fascinating Husqvarnas are the 456cc Desert Master and Cross Country, a pair of off-road monsters that are capable of turning brave men into ashen ghosts with one injudicious twist of the wrist. So much power—46 hp—is waiting for the unwary that even the Husky's excellent frame and suspension can be overtaxed. In the hands of expert class riders, the 450s can cover grueling distances in events like the Baja 1000 faster than nearly anything else. But unless you've got muscles of iron and nerves of steel, you'd better not get too close to a big Husky.

Husqvarna 450

Engine: Two-stroke Single
8.8:1 compression ratio, 84x82mm, 456cc
Ignition: Capacitive discharge
Transmission: 5-speed **Wheelbase:** 54 in
Ground Clearance: 8.75 in **Weight:** 249 lbs

Kawasaki

Premier

Premier Enduro 125

Engine: Two-stroke Single
11:1 compression ratio, 54x54mm, 124cc
Ignition: Flywheel magneto
Transmission: 5-speed **Wheelbase:** 51 in
Ground Clearance: 7.5 in **Weight:** 206 lbs.

The Premier 125 is actually a Moto Beta, imported by Berliner Motors and christened after one of its divisions. Alongside the Ducatis, Moto Guzzis and Nortons that Berliner stocks, the Premier looks a bit out of place, for it's a typical Italian dual-purpose machine similar to the Benelli 175.

Almost everything about the bike is perfectly straightforward, from the 124cc two-stroke Single to the 21-inch front wheel and pre-mix fuel. Not of competition caliber—its top speed is 60 mph—the Premier is still a solid and relatively inexpensive playbike that's street-legal, attractive and fairly reliable.

There is also a Penton Trials 125, meant to compete with the Spanish marques. This is built in England, though the engine comes from Sachs. The frame is chrome-moly, and the rest of the equipment is championship caliber. Pentons don't yet dominate trials the way they do the ISDT enduros, but maybe that will come, too. For now, the Pentons are the best small-bore machines for ISDT competition, bar none.

Penton Hare Scrambler 250

Engine: Two-stroke Single
14.1 compression ratio, 71x62mm, 246cc
Ignition: Capacitive discharge
Transmission: 6-speed   **Wheelbase:** 55 in
Ground Clearance: 9 in   **Weight:** 212 lbs

calculated for the highest efficiency on smooth dirt tracks. The Stiletto will broadside easily, and with optimum control. That's what's needed for TT racing, and that's why it wins.

The second 250 Ossa—and most highly tuned after the Stiletto—is the Six Day Replica. The SDR is meant to be an ISDT bike, producing more horsepower than the enduro-type Pioneer, but greater flexibility than the full-race Stiletto. The suspension is by Betor, the alloy rims by Akront and the carburetor a special model from Amal. The SDR is basically a high-performance enduro bike, fitted with street-legal equipment but intended for off-road competition.

Ossa Stiletto 250 TT
Engine: Two-stroke Single
14.1:1 compression ratio, 72x60mm, 244cc
Ignition: Capacitive discharge
Transmission: 5-speed **Wheelbase:** 55 in
Ground Clearance: 6 in **Weight:** 225 lbs

Very similar to the SDR is the Ossa Pioneer, an excellent enduro bike in the same Spanish idiom as Bultaco's Alpina and Montesa's Cappra. The 250cc Single yields a few less horsepower than the more highly stressed SDR unit, but it's also got better low-speed torque and reliability. All it really lacks is an automatic oil-injection system. A 21-inch front wheel, Pirelli knobbies and Betor suspension make it work well in the rough.

The Pioneer is considered one of the easiest bikes to ride fast in tough terrain. Street-legal accessories are included, but they're marginal at best, meant for fulfilling the letter of the law rather than providing truly usable components. But that doesn't matter; few riders would want to use the Pioneer anywhere but off-road anyway, for that's where it excels.

Ossa Pioneer/SDR 250

Engine: Two-stroke Single
13.1:1 compression ratio, 72x60mm, 244cc
Ignition: Capacitive discharge
Transmission: 5-speed **Wheelbase:** 55 in
Ground Clearance: 11 in **Weight:** 235 lbs

The slowest of all the Ossa 250s is also the best at what it does. The Plonker is a championship-quality trials bike, equaled only by the Bultaco Sherpa T and Montesa Cota 247. There is really little to choose from among the three Spanish bikes for serious trials competition, for all are similar solutions to the same problem.

The Plonker comes with a strong, torquey Single, Betor suspension, Akront rims, Pirelli tires, steel fenders and a fiberglass tank. It has functional and rather lovely styling, but slightly less ground clearance than the equivalent Bultaco.

Ossa Plonker 250

Engine: Two-stroke Single
9.5:1 compression ratio, 72x60mm, 244cc
Ignition: Capacitive discharge
Transmission: 5-speed **Wheelbase:** 51 in
Ground Clearance: 10.5 in **Weight:** 203 lbs

Penton

Penton Six Day 125

Engine: Two-stroke Single
10:1 compression ratio, 54x54mm, 123cc
Ignition: Capacitive discharge
Transmission: 6-speed **Wheelbase:** 55 in
Ground Clearance: 9 in **Weight:** 210 lbs

John Penton and his family are among the best off-road riders in the country. After years of riding other people's machines, they determined to ride their own. The bikes are actually built in Austria by KTM, and use either 125cc engines built by Sachs or 175cc Singles made by KTM itself. All Pentons are basically identical, with the option of lighting equipment to make an enduro model, or number plates to create a motocrosser. There are also new 250cc enduro and motocross Pentons with KTM engines and chassis similar to the smaller models.

Penton motorcycles—like the Penton family—excel in arduous enduros like the ISDT qualifiers and the ISDT itself. The U.S. team is usually mounted on Pentons, while hundreds of other less skillful enduro riders buy Pentons because they know that it's one of the best machines around.

Ossa

Ossa has been building bikes for nearly three decades, and has been successful in most forms of two-wheel competition over the years. The present line is formed around one engine/frame combination which functions well in virtually all off-road situations. There is a lone 175cc version of the basic machine, but all the rest of the extensive Ossa line are 250s.

For the very specialized world of TT racing, Ossa builds its Stiletto TT. This comes as a race-ready machine out of the box, complete with engine and frame modified to Dick Mann's suggestions. It makes 36 hp and has provision for an optional compression release. Number plates are standard, and the frame geometry is

Some of the Cota components also appear on the 125cc and 250cc Montesa Cappra motocross bikes, but these machines are engineered for the tough, high-speed world of international motocross competition rather than the quiet precision of trials. Chrome-moly frames, plastic fenders, Akront rims, stainless steel spokes and Pirelli tires are just some of the quality components that Montesa uses to ensure competitive performance. Both bikes provide ample amounts of horsepower from their two-stroke Singles, and both handle well.

These attributes are shared by the new Montesa King Scorpion, the 250cc enduro model with street-legal lighting equipment. This incorporates an automatic oil injection unit, unlike the racers which require premixed fuel. Most of the running gear on the King Scorpion is shared with the Cappra racers, making the enduro a highly competent woods bike indeed.

Montesa Cappra 250VR
Engine: Two-stroke Single
12:1 compression ratio, 70x64mm, 246cc
Ignition: Capacitive discharge
Transmission: 5-speed **Wheelbase:** 55 in
Ground Clearance: 8.5 in **Weight:** 219 lbs

Montesa

Montesa assembles a line of five machines using one basic configuration, modified to supply different displacements and motorcycles for different specific purposes. There are two trials bikes—the Cota 123 and Cota 247—and both are championship material.

Among the lightest of all trialers, the Montesas feature good power and excellent handling. The one-piece fiberglass seat and tank combination is beautifully styled, a revelation in a field where machinery is judged on how it performs rather than how it looks. But if the mechanical end of things is well taken care of, then time is left to be concerned about styling and such subtle refinements as an automatic chain lubricant reservoir on the swing arm and neatly indented cases on the engine so that the footpegs can be tucked in for greater clearance in narrow passages. It's attention to detail that keeps Montesa on top in trials.

Montesa Cota 123

Engine: Two-stroke Single
12:1 compression ratio, 54x54mm, 123cc
Ignition: Flywheel magneto
Transmission: 6-speed **Wheelbase:** 48 in
Ground Clearance: 11 in **Weight:** 157 lbs

A limited line of high-quality, pure racing machines comes from this small West German family-owned factory, and it simply dominates motocross in many countries. The smallest bike is a 125cc, but the most important are the 250 and 400. These have top-quality components like Reynolds drive chains, Girling shocks and unbreakable fiberglass fenders coupled with two-stroke Singles that produce great amounts of horsepower. The 400, for example, is rated at 41 hp, and the frame is sturdy enough to get a good portion of that to the ground most of the time. The radial finning on the head keeps temperatures down, so Maicos tend to run as long as they run fast.

Nearly everything on the 250 and 400 Maicos, except the engine, is identical to that on the mind-boggling 501cc, 48 hp Brobdingnagian mount that Maico claims is just about the fastest way around any off-road course. Even more than other big racers like the 450 Husqvarna and 500 Yamaha, the 501 Maico is too much bike for anyone but international motocross stars—it's positively awesome in its conversion of brute force into forward motion.

Maico

Maico 501

Engine: Two-stroke Single
12:1 compression ratio, 91.6x76mm, 501cc
Ignition: Flywheel magneto
Transmission: 4-speed **Wheelbase:** 56 in
Ground Clearance: 10 in **Weight:** 242 lbs

Maico 400 Motocross

Engine: Two-stroke Single
12:1 compression ratio, 77x83mm, 387cc
Ignition: Flywheel magneto
Transmission: 4-speed **Wheelbase:** 56 in
Ground Clearance: 7.5 in **Weight** 228 lbs

Kawasaki 250

Engine: Two-stroke Single
7.1:1 compression ratio, 68x68mm, 247cc
Ignition: Flywheel magneto
Transmission: 5-speed **Wheelbase:** 55 in
Ground Clearance: 8 in **Weight:** 270 lbs

The best Kawasaki dirt bike is also one of the best, period. The F-11 250cc enduro has the same infinitely adjustable suspension featured on the 175. It also has a full-floating back plate on the rear brake that provides better braking on loose surfaces. The wheel rims are alloy, the styling is pleasant and the handling is more than adequate. There is also a positive stop in the transmission that prevents overshifting or false neutrals. When tire adhesion is most important on slippery terrain, confidence that the next gear you get is the one you wanted can be a welcome bonus. Street-legal equipment makes the F-11 into a dual-purpose machine, but its real home is still definitely off the highway.

The best Kawasaki dirt bike is also one of the best, period. The F-11 250cc enduro has the same infinitely adjustable suspension featured on the 175. It also has a full-floating back plate on the rear brake that provides better braking on loose surfaces. The wheel rims are alloy, the styling is pleasant and the handling is more than adequate. There is also a positive stop in the transmission that prevents overshifting or false neutrals. When tire adhesion is most important on slippery terrain, confidence that the next gear you get is the one you wanted can be a welcome bonus. Street-legal equipment makes the F-11 into a dual-purpose machine, but its real home is still definitely off the highway.

Kawasaki 250

Engine: Two-stroke Single
7.1:1 compression ratio, 68x68mm, 247cc
Ignition: Flywheel magneto
Transmission: 5-speed **Wheelbase:** 55 in
Ground Clearance: 8 in **Weight:** 270 lbs

Kawasaki has slightly less variety in its dirt bike line than the other Japanese manufacturers, with only five dual-purpose machines intended for trail riding. Two 100cc trail bikes—one with a dual-range transmission that gives an effective 10-speed gearbox—constitute the bottom rung. Kawasaki's first true dirt bike is the 125cc F-6, which develops more horsepower than any other bike its size. The front suspension can be adjusted to various positions, and fork spring tension can even be controlled.

Everything about the 125 Kawasaki is quite refined, and the larger 175cc F-7 is the same, only more so. This one features five-way adjustable rear shocks, while the front forks can be raised or lowered in the triple clamps and the sliders can be rotated to provide three different axle positions. The spring rates are also alterable. The 175 is as powerful as most 250s, as sophisticated as any machine on the market and as pretty as a dirt bike can be. Although modified versions make successful racers, it's more a pleasant trail-riding companion than a racing competitor. Then again, most riders aren't full-bore racers, either.

Kawasaki 175

Engine: Two-stroke Single
7.1:1 compression ratio, 61.5x59mm, 174cc
Ignition: Capacitive discharge
Transmission: 5-speed **Wheelbase:** 52 in
Ground Clearance: 10 in **Weight:** 233 lbs

Suzuki

Suzuki Sierra 185

Engine: Two-stroke Single
6.7:1 compression ratio, 64x57mm, 183cc
Ignition: Capacitive discharge
Transmission: 5-speed **Wheelbase:** 52.5 in
Ground Clearance: 9 in **Weight:** 218 lbs

Suzuki has an unusual group of off-road bikes, with five tiny dual-purpose machines under 125cc at the bottom end of the scale and two potent 400cc monsters of championship caliber. In between, a mix of street-oriented dirt bikes and motocross racers provide something for novices and experts, but leave the merely competent dirt rider looking elsewhere.

There is a slick 125 motocross racer with almost all the options needed to make a successful competitor, and the price is considerably lower than for many other racing mounts. Next is the Sierra 185, a dual-purpose playbike that features most of the amenities—automatic oiling, adjustable suspension, high exhaust and skid plate. It surely won't win any races, but it handles well enough for fooling around, it's street-legal and it's quite attractive.

of street bikes. An all-position carburetor will keep the engine running even if it's upside down, and Betor suspension units provide extravagantly good handling.

The unusual two-stroke Single has a rope-pull starter like that on a snowmobile, and also a Salisbury torque converter that eliminates transmission gears. This functions as an infinitely variable automatic transmission—like that in DAF cars—with the gear ratio always perfectly selected for the amount of engine torque needed. It works so well that you can expect to see it on lots of other bikes—both off-road and street machines—in the near future. The other marques will be copying the Rokon, easily the most innovative bike on the market right now.

Rokon RT-340
Engine: Two-stroke Single
11.8:1 compression ratio, 78x70mm, 340cc
Ignition: Flywheel magneto
Transmission: Variable ratio **Wheelbase:** 56 in
Ground Clearance: 10 in **Weight:** 260 lbs

Rokon

Built by a tiny company in Keene, New Hampshire, the Rokon 340 may just revolutionize two-wheel design. Until now, Rokon has been known as the manufacturer of Trail-Breakers—the ugliest and also the most effective two-wheel off-road vehicles made. These come with all-wheel-drive, giant low-psi tractor tires and a variable-ratio automatic transmission. The Rokon 340 is pretty compared to Trail-Breakers, but it's equally unconventional.

To start with, it has cast alloy wheels. There are no spokes, and thus none to come loose . . . or to adjust. Mounted on these snow-flake wheels are hydraulic disc brakes front and rear—which give the Rokon the best brakes of any dirt bike. It will even outstop a lot haps that's why the price is so steep. But it's also part of the reason that Rickmans are among the most beautiful of all dirt bikes, with their pale blue fiberglass tanks, seats and fenders and those shiny frames. There are two 125cc models—with Zundapp engines—that are identical except for the street-legal accessories on the Enduro and the number plates on the Motocross. A similar 250cc Motocross with a Montesa engine fills out the line.

All three bikes have Betor forks and Girling shocks, waterproof boots over the levers, throttle and carburetor, a waterproof air-cleaner chamber and automatic chain oilers. All are built exclusively for competition, and all have excellent handling. If you're really serious about motocross competition, the Rickmans are about as serious as you can get.

Rickman

Rickman 125

Engine: Two-stroke Single
11:1 compression ratio, 54x54mm, 123cc
Ignition: Flywheel magneto
Transmission: 5-speed **Wheelbase:** 53 in
Ground Clearance: 10 in **Weight:** 216 lbs

Don and Derek Rickman are championship motocross riders turned manufacturers. A decade ago, they found that none of the machines available were quite what they needed, so they went into limited production of specials on a backyard basis. Later, there were some road racers and café racers with excellent handling, and later still, a tie-in with the strike-plagued BSA/Triumph conglomerate. Rickman dirt bikes are now distributed by Triumph, and thousands a year come off the assembly lines.

From the very beginning, Rickmans had nickel-plated frames as a distinguishing trademark, and the custom is still adhered to. Per-

Puch

Puch Enduro 125
Engine: Two-stroke Single
11.5:1 compression ratio, 55x52mm, 124cc
Ignition: Capacitive discharge
Transmission: 5-speed **Wheelbase:** 54 in
Ground Clearance: 11.5 in **Weight:** 209 lbs

One of the oldest of all motorcycle firms, the Austrian Puch factory started turning out machines in 1899. Nowdays they sell two 125cc and two 175cc models in this country, all built around the same chassis components. There is an enduro model and a motocrosser in each category, identical except for lighting equipment on the enduro.

The 125 has an excellent record in ISDT competition, as successful and reliable as the Pentons. The gearbox is a little weak—also a Penton failing—but other than that, the Puch 125 is solid as can be. As in most competition bikes, oil has to be added to the fuel, but Betor forks, Girling rear shocks, Metzeler tires, alloy rims and numerous small, high-quality parts are used on all the Puchs.

Right in the middle of the Suzuki pack is the 250. This two-stroke Single is a perfect playbike—excellent handling, good ground clearance, automatic oil injection, high exhaust, knobby tires and a skid plate. It's a bit heavy for serious dirt use, but as a dual-purpose machine it can't be beat. The price is right, the styling is good and the performance is more than adequate for keeping up with traffic. Top speed is over 80 mph. Of course, low-speed pulling power suffers because of the high gearing, but the Savage isn't intended for tight spots in any case.

For going really fast on a motocross track, the 250cc racing version is the answer. Joel Robert has had fantastic success on Suzuki's factory bikes in international motocross competition, and his bikes aren't all that different from the ones Suzuki sells. And then there's the 400. This has been the bike to beat in international 500-class competition, and many of the features found on the factory racers are retained on the production motocross versions. The TM-400 and dual-purpose TS-400 are a lot easier to handle than some other big-bore dirt bikes, and they do most everything with uncomplicated dispatch. All the Suzukis share that happy characteristic.

Suzuki GT-250

Engine: Two-stroke Single
6.7:1 compression ratio, 70x64mm, 246cc
Ignition: Capacitive discharge
Transmission: 5-speed **Wheelbase:** 56 in
Ground Clearance: 8 in **Weight:** 245 lbs

Triumph

Triumph Avenger 500

Engine: Four-stroke Single
9:1 compression ratio, 84x90mm, 499cc
Ignition: Capacitive discharge
Transmission: 4-speed **Wheelbase:** 54 in
Ground Clearance: 7.5 in **Weight:** 260 lbs

Although besieged in England by money and production problems, Triumph continues to serve as a bastion of four-stroke technology. There are two Triumph 500cc dirt bikes available—the Avenger and the Trophy Trail. They share frames and sundry parts, but feature two different engines.

The Triumph Avenger is the old BSA 440 Victor punched out to an honest 500cc and wearing fancy new trim. All the off-road necessities are included—skid plate, number plates, knobby tires, Girling shocks, long-travel front forks—and there are some new touches as well: witness the one-into-two exhaust system and positive swing-arm adjuster plates. It's a bit overweight, but there is a race-kit that makes the old thumper go surprisingly well. And if you still love the sound of a big four-stroke Single echoing through the woods, there's no help for you but a Triumph.

Triumph's other dirt bike is basically the same machine as the Avenger, but with the old 500cc Triumph Twin shoehorned into the Victor frame. It's completely street-legal, and has full instrumentation. The single-carb Twin feeds two exhausts into one pipe that snakes out the bottom, making it one of the quietest dirt bikes around. Immense amounts of torque are on tap, especially under street riding conditions, where the Trophy Trail excels. It's really too heavy for a dirt bike in the form delivered, but back in the old days, remember, Triumph Twins ruled the deserts and the woods. That won't happen again, but there are certainly enough old-timers who'd like to see it come to pass.

Triumph Trophy Trail 500

Engine: Four-stroke Twin
9:1 compression ratio, 69x65.5mm, 490cc
Ignition: Battery and coil
Transmission: 4-speed **Wheelbase:** 54 in
Ground Clearance: 7.5 in **Weight:** 330 lbs

Yamaha has one of the most complete dirt bike lines in the world. It starts with enduro and motocross versions of the 100cc LT3 and then goes to enduro, motocross and trials versions of the 125. The 125 enduro even has an electric starter, and all the rest of the accessories you need for a worry-free, dual-purpose playbike.

The motocross version is competitive in its class, and while not overwhelming championship material, is a solid, dependable machine that won't do anything unexpected. The trials 125 is very similar. You won't compete in the expert class with champions on Bultacos and Ossas, but then, most riders—let alone machines—aren't up to that sort of test.

Yamaha

Yamaha AT Enduro 125

Engine: Two-stroke Single
7:1 compression ratio, 56x50mm, 123cc
Ignition: Capacitive discharge
Transmission: 5-speed **Wheelbase:** 51 in
Ground Clearance: 9 in **Weight:** 220 lbs

Yamaha's reputation for building high-quality dirt bikes rests primarily on its 250s. There is a 175 enduro, and it's a fine dual-purpose machine, but the interest centers on the 125s and 250s. The DT3 250 enduro has been in production for about eight years, and it just doesn't need changing. It comes with almost anything you could need on a playbike—autolube, resettable odometer, 21-inch front wheel—and with some of the weighty accessories stripped off, makes a competitive enduro racer.

The motocross version of the 250 is equally good, although it's not very similar to the factory machines that win so many races. Things like alloy rims, spool-type hubs, autolube and a high exhaust mean a quick, reliable racer that is relatively maintenance-free. It's a fine mount for medium-grade motocross racing, and while you won't win many championships on a Yamaha MX, you also won't spend most of your off-track time in the shop. Whether you need something more potent depends on how seriously you take your racing. Most people will be content with this one.

Yamaha DT Enduro 250
Engine: Two-stroke Single
6.8:1 compression ratio, 70x64mm, 246cc
Ignition: Flywheel magneto
Transmission: 5-speed **Wheelbase:** 55 in
Ground Clearance: 8 in **Weight:** 260 lbs

Yamaha's new trials bike is equally reliable—and easy to maintain. It has automatic oil injection to save you the mess of mixing fuel . . . and that's almost worth the price of admission right there. Styling on the trials machine is subtle and fine, ground clearance is ample, and handling is competitive. There is a lot of low-speed torque on hand, a massive skid plate and a light alloy front end to get you through the tight spots as easily as possible. Like all Yamahas, it's a good, solid motorcycle that won't let you down.

Yamaha Trials 250

Engine: Two-stroke Single
6.8:1 compression ratio, 70x64mm, 246cc
Ignition: Flywheel magneto
Transmission: 5-speed **Wheelbase:** 55 in
Ground Clearance: 10 in **Weight:** 220 lbs

Very similar to the 250s, the 351cc Enduro and MX Yamahas share many of the same characteristics, if not the actual parts. Reed-valve induction makes this one of the strongest engines in its class, while rotating counterweights beneath the crankshaft dampen out vibration. A polypropylene front fender, tuck-away exhaust, electronic ignition and clean styling make the 360 one of the best dual-purpose bikes available. And the top speed is over 80 mph.

The Yamaha MX 360 motocross racer features plastic fenders, aluminum wheel rims, lightened frame and alloy components wherever possible. There is even autolube, to eliminate the mess of fuel mixing. Although it differs in many respects from the factory motocross team bikes, the production MX 360 is still a competitive racer at all but the highest levels of competition.

If you must test yourself at the top level, there is always the 496cc two-stroke Single. This is basically a bored-out 360 that develops some 44 hp at 6500 rpm—or just about enough to terrify anyone. Like most other 500-class motocross racers, this one is definitely for experts only. It will accelerate like a dragster, handle like a racer and win like nothing else.

Yamaha RT Enduro 360

Engine: Two-stroke Single
6.3:1 compression ratio, 80x70mm, 351cc
Ignition: Capacitive discharge
Transmission: 5-speed **Wheelbase:** 55 in
Ground Clearance: 9 in **Weight:** 262 lbs